The Prairie Fire

The Prairie Fire

written by MARILYNN REYNOLDS

illustrated by DON KILBY

ORCA BOOK PUBLISHERS

There was a time when terrible fires swept for miles across the prairie. The fires started in spring and fall, when the land was dry, and they burned the grasses, the trees, the sod houses and everything in their path.

"Watch for a cloud of smoke in the sky," Father told Percy one fall afternoon. "If a prairie fire's coming, that's the first thing you'll see. And if a high wind's blowing, that fire will race across the prairie faster than wild horses."

Mother reached over and took Percy's hand. "Maybe there won't be any fires this year," she said. But her eyes looked worried. It was already the beginning of October, and the grass around the homestead was as parched as straw.

"Tomorrow I'll start to plow a fireguard around the house and barn," Father said wearily. "If a prairie fire comes this way, there'll be no grass for it to burn and it'll pass us by."

Percy looked at Father's heavy shoulders, his sunburned neck, and his big scarred fingers. "I can plow too," he said.

But Father shook his head. "You can help me when you're bigger."

That night Percy dreamed about the fire running with the wind. Running as fast as a galloping horse. Racing straight toward their house with nothing to stop it.

Early next morning Father got up in the dark and went out to the barn to hitch the oxen — Old Jim and Frank — to the plow. All week Percy watched as his father and the oxen plowed a giant circle around the house, the barn and the haystacks. Every day the circle of plowed land grew wider.

"The fireguard's almost twenty yards across," Father said with satisfaction at supper one night. "If a fire heads this way, there'll be hardly a blade of grass to burn around the homestead." He smiled. "I'll plow one last round tomorrow, then I think we'll be safe."

"I'm big enough," Percy said the next day. "Can't I help Dad plow the last part of the fireguard?"

His mother shook her head. "Maybe another year, when you're older." She smiled at his sad face. "Why don't you go out and feed Maud?"

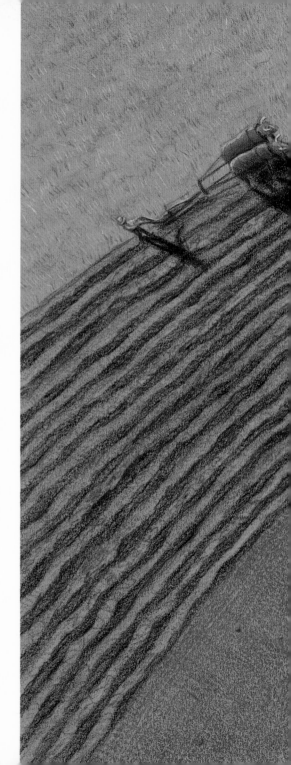

Percy slowly trudged across the yard to the barn. Maud's white coat gleamed in the dark. He breathed in the sweet smell of the mare's sweat and stroked her neck. "Dad thinks I'm too little to help," he said. Maud chewed the hay with her big teeth and whinnied softly.

When Maud finished, Percy left the barn and ran across the fireguard and out onto the prairie. All around him, the land stretched brown in the October sunshine. It was strangely empty. The crows, blackbirds and robins had flown south, and the gophers were deep in their holes underground. Silence lay everywhere.

A cold, brisk breeze stirred the grass. Percy heard a noise like a pack of barking dogs. He looked up. Overhead, in a long wavy vee, a flock of late-migrating geese was traveling to warmer lands. Percy's heart soared with the birds as they grew smaller and farther away.

And that's when he saw it. A bluish-black cloud to the southeast.

Even as Percy watched, the cloud grew larger and larger. Suddenly he realized that it wasn't an ordinary cloud.

It was smoke — smoke from a prairie fire.

Somewhere, miles away, lightning had lit the grasses. Or a settler's campfire had escaped. Now a prairie fire was running across the land with a high wind at its back, burning everything in its path.

Percy sank to his knees and stared at the black cloud. He couldn't move. He felt frozen to the grass.

Then Percy sprang to his feet. He raced back to the fireguard. "Dad!" he shouted as he ran. "Smoke! I see smoke!"

Percy's father got off the plow and squinted at the horizon. "Help me unyoke the oxen," he said quietly.

As Percy and his father worked, Old Jim and Frank began to move about uneasily. Old Jim sniffed the air and tossed his head from side to side. Frank pawed the ground.

"They smell the smoke," his father said.

When the oxen were free, Father whacked them on the rump. "Save yourselves, boys!" he shouted, as the pair stumbled off across the prairie toward the water in the slough.

Leaving the plow where it stood, Father and Percy ran back to the homestead. "Fire!" they shouted as Mother rushed out of the house. "A fire's coming!"

The smell of smoke was stronger now. When Percy and his father reached the barn, they found Maud bolting around in her stall. Father tried to quiet the mare as he led her out into the yard. She danced nervously while he hitched her to the flat stoneboat. Quickly he led the horse to the rain barrel beside the house. Father heaved the barrel, heavy with rainwater, onto the stoneboat and thrust an empty pail into Percy's hands.

"You and Maud will have to guard the haystacks and the buildings," Father said. "If sparks land here, douse them with water. Mother and I'll go to the fireguard and put out any sparks that land there."

"Don't go!" Percy cried, hanging onto his father's arm. Percy hung his head. "I'm afraid of the fire," he whispered.

His father hugged Percy tight to his chest. And his mother kissed him. But there was no time to waste. Gathering up all the gunnysacks they could find, his parents ran out to the fireguard. Percy and the horse were left alone in the yard.

Percy's nose and eyes stung from the smoke as the fire came closer. Within minutes the hissing and crackling flames reached the homestead. Showers of sparks sailed over the fireguard and dropped into the barnyard.

"Come on, Maud!" In the flickering red light of the fire, Percy pulled Maud over to the sparks. Sometimes the smoke was so thick and the air so hot that he could scarcely breathe. But he led Maud around the yard, pulling the rain barrel to places where the sparks landed and dousing them with his pail of water.

Then, to Percy's amazement, two rabbits and a coyote ran into the yard to escape the flames. When the terrified animals ran past Percy's feet, Maud started. She began to kick, and the precious barrel of rainwater rocked back and forth on the stoneboat. Maud screamed, and for the first time in his life, Percy was afraid of her. He tried to calm the mare, but Maud reared high above him. Water sloshed out of the rain barrel, and the horse's reins swung out of Percy's reach.

"Dad! Dad, help me!" he shouted. Through the smoke he could see his parents against the orange sky, beating out the sparks. He could hear them shouting to each other. But in the noise of the fire they couldn't hear him.

Again and again Percy jumped up to grab Maud's reins. But Maud kept twisting her head away. At last Percy ran to the barn. He came back with his arms full of hay and laid it before the rearing horse.

At the sight of the hay, Maud quieted. She bent her head and took a mouthful. With trembling fingers, Percy undid the buttons of his old cotton shirt and pulled it off his shoulders. As the mare ate, he tied the shirt across her eyes like a bandage.

Percy grabbed the reins and pulled the blindfolded horse toward the small fires that had started up in the farmyard. At first Maud whinnied and pulled back, but finally she shuddered and followed him.

Back and forth they went, from the haystacks to the barn and to the sod house. Back and forth until there were fewer and fewer fires to put out.

At last there were none. With a rush of hot air, the prairie fire passed by the homestead.

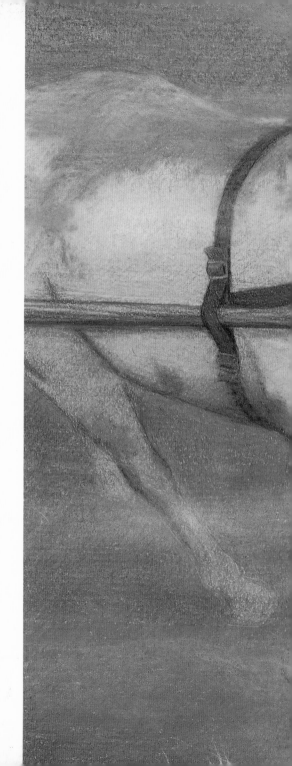

Percy's mother and father came through the smoke and staggered, coughing, into the farmyard. Their eyes were red and their faces and clothes black with charred grass and soot. When they saw Percy through the haze, they ran to him, and the family clung together in the smoking yard.

Late that afternoon, Percy and his parents stood in the doorway of the sod house. Curls of smoke drifted up around the haystacks and little fires still smouldered along the fireguard. Out on the prairie, the path of the fire was charred black to the edge of the sky.

"Do you think Old Jim and Frank are all right?" Percy asked, anxiously.

Father put his arm around Percy's shoulders. "They had plenty of time to reach the slough, and they probably waded out into the water where the fire couldn't reach them. Those boys are a pretty smart pair. They must be hungry by now. I think I'll walk down to the slough and drive them back to the barn."

Father looked down at Percy and smiled. "It's a job for two men. Why don't you come with me, Son? I'll need your help."

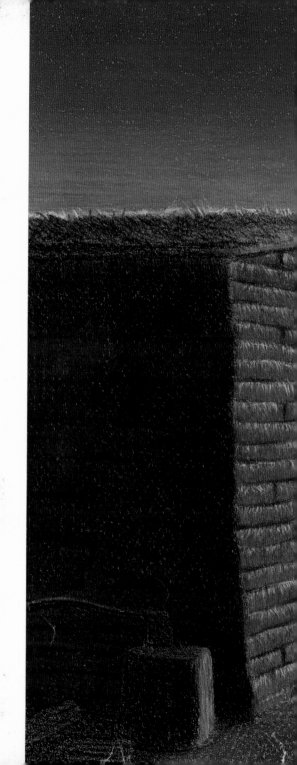

Canadian Cataloguing in Publication Data
Reynolds, Marilynn, 1940 –
The prairie fire

ISBN 1-55143-137-8

1. Grassland fires — Juvenile fiction.   2. Frontier and pioneer life — Prairie Provinces —
Juvenile fiction.
I. Kilby, Don.   II. Title.
PS8585.E973P72 1999 jC813'.54 C99-910040-8
PZ7.R33735Pr 1999

Library of Congress Catalog Card Number: 98-89928

Orca Book Publishers gratefully acknowledges the
support of our publishing programs provided by the following agencies: the
Department of Canadian Heritage, The Canada Council for the Arts, and the British
Columbia Arts Council.

Design by Christine Toller

Printed and bound in Hong Kong

Orca Book Publishers   **Orca Book Publishers**
PO Box 5626, Station B   PO Box 468
Victoria, BC Canada   Custer, WA   USA
V8R 6S4   98240-0468

99 00 01   5 4 3 2 1